Dragon Dreams

Dragon Dreams

*Ruth,
I hope you enjoy this as much as I did writing it.
Keep Safe.
Love
[signature]*

Richard G. Evans

Copyright © 2010 by Richard G. Evans.

ISBN: Softcover   978-1-4500-6639-6
           EBook   978-1-4500-6640-2

All rights reserved. No part of this book may be reproduced or transmitted in any form or by any means, electronic or mechanical, including photocopying, recording, or by any information storage and retrieval system, without permission in writing from the copyright owner.

This is a work of fiction. Names, characters, places and incidents either are the product of the author's imagination or are used fictitiously, and any resemblance to any actual persons, living or dead, events, or locales is entirely coincidental.

This book was printed in the United States of America.

To order additional copies of this book, contact:
Xlibris Corporation
1-888-795-4274
www.Xlibris.com
Orders@Xlibris.com
78519

CONTENTS

DRAGONS DREAM

The Silence of the Mind 13
Chapter Two 17
Chapter Three 25

THE DRAGON AND THE MINERS

A Time to Remember 45
Chapter Two. 49
Chapter Three 53

Reason To Believe In 57
Chapter Two 61
Chapter Three 63

A Dragons Tale 67

Stories of Dragons who, along with the Angels, watch over you. with Love and Joy that is given to them by GOD, who so loves us all that HE Gave to us HIS Only Begotten Son.

In all who live, there will at times be pain and adversity. But know that GOD, HIS Angels and Dragons Love you. That Dragons fight for you and will and do die for you. That all that matters to Dragons is to Love, Serve and Die for GOD!

DRAGON STORIES
BY
RICHARD G. EVANS

Dedication.

These stories are dedicated to my Much Beloved Wife, Pauline Marie.

Who and always shall be an inspiration to me!

She makes everything right!

I also dedicate these stories to my Wondrous Sister Christine, who is always in our Thoughts and Hearts!

My Wife & my Sister are true Graces from GOD!

DRAGONS DREAM

by
Richard Glyndwr Evans

Oh how I yearn to rest beside the river as it plies it's coolness to far reaches. To bathe in it's lushness as the water caresses me and cradles me too the sea.

But now, sadness is my lot!

For I must await my fate in the shadows of the mind whilst others gambol upon the soil that I once did freely tread.

I look too the skies and see the clouds that I did frolic in as a pup. But now I am chained too the reality of my being.

For I am to serve those who would have me do harm to others less expecting of such.

'GO HERE'! They in their panic do yell at me!

'GET YOU THERE'! They do shout at me!

'KILL THESE OUR MORTAL FOES'! Do they command of me!

Oh! for the peace that will cover my body and save me, wretched creature that am I, from the continual death and destruction that I am commanded to reap upon such hapless souls that abound this Earth.

Oh how I wish that I could look too the sun one more time and see people live and play freely and kindly as did once my own had done.

But I am lost now to them who were, for I am the last and I am deserted by life of joy!

And condemned to the iniquity of this life of Hell!!

Again I go forth to do the bidding of those who can do nought for themselves but tremble.

But I have never wanted to kill, nor to cause pain or distress, and yet I know that I do cause by my ugliness fear and unrelenting distrust and incomprehension of my kind does abound.

Upon my return to these people who so fondly sit so smug in their houses drinking their wine, gratified in their misplaced knowledge that I have dispatched their enemies with but a sweep of my tail or a beat of my wings. Or that I have consumed them with the heat and flames of my breath. That I have torn and mangled to shreds the miserable bodies of their enemies, and scattered them to dust. Or worse! That I have eaten their rotting carcasses and then strewn the bones as like feed for the carrion.

But no! None of these things have I done.

For the arrival in pomp and majesty of such as I has confounded the enemy. And I have striven to make them friends.

Oh sadness does entrap me as I still may see only the futility of the strife that is abundant.

And so I sit beside this river and hope that my release will come and I will join with my own once again.

THE SILENCE OF THE MIND

by
Richard Glyndwr Evans

As the waters of the river wind steadily by, sweeping all that falls too it's surface along with it in an urgency that it alone knows, I sit by it's side watching as the World unfurls it's knowledge too me in silence. And in silence I absorb and learn.

But the weight of life and memories is heavy upon me and my soul cries out in anguish and pain as I take repose. But there is no rest or peace for such as I.

No! There can only be pain, anguish and suffering. For time and life is of such a magnitude of indifference to such as I that my ignominy is of such little consequence that naught of attentions by passers-by are conveyed towards me.

My existence is but a whim of their imaginations that are but fleeting glimpses into their being. And soon they are gone and I remain in silent repose.

Steadily the wind does rise as the clouds ramble in too cover the dwindling blue sky in all their majesty as the time rolls away and slowly day becomes night.

The clouds take command and the Moon in rising struggles vainly too cast the afterglow of the passing sun onto the face of the Earth.

And still I remain.

For there is naught for me to energize over. All is at peace and such as I are not called upon to wage battle for others.

And so it is with a sadness that I rest my head and think of my existence upon this Earth. And I recall the joy at encountering people who beseeched such as I to come too them, only for me to feel the horrors of their revulsion and scorn that was eventually heaped upon such liken too myself.

And so I sit here in silence as I listen too the continuing chatter of the river as it wends away from me.

I remain and wait for my last breath and dream of the peace that is never to be mine.

I wait for the Angel of Death to take my last breath away with naught but a scant look back at my slumped body. And for me to become chilled by the Angels scorn towards me.

But throughout the night there is no sign of my death.

And so I must remain too serve all who bid me too do their will.

And in turn for me to be in receipt of their abuse and revulsion at the sight of my existence.

Oh that I could be given release. That I may stay by the river and dream and never have to fight again.

But that will never be.

Slowly the dark clouds give way too greyness as the sun rises, enshrouded by the morning cloudy sky.

I listen too the river, but all is still around.

I look and see people moving towards me. At first I see their stiffening as they espy my prone figure.

Steadily, as before they cross away from me. Averted from me are their gazes, as they fuss with one-another in an effort to ignore me.

To obliterate me from their sight and mind.

So! Slowly as the morning begins I slowly rise. I gather my belongings before I arrange my weapons. The people near me rush to depart from me.

Slowly but steadily there comes a man of the Church.

I overt my eyes, for I am unworthy to look upon him. He faltered in his step as he neared me.

For a moment his gaze met mine as he looked up at my face. But there was nothing he could see as my helmet and visor covered my head and face.

Suddenly there was a darkening of his face as he looked at my armoured body.

And the realization that he was standing in front of something that he had no desire to be near over-took him with alacrity and he suddenly jerked away from me and his step quickened as he rushed to away from my being.

Slowly a smile crept across my mouth as I watched him join the scurrying throng, who seemed to be so pre-occupied with escaping the vicinity of my being.

I then turned and steadily walked into the town.

I saw people rush away and I heard doors crashing shut as I neared them.

From all the windows I saw peering faces. Faces full of hatred and fear.

Faces of people who had earlier beckoned me too them with open arms.

But who now wished for nothing more than for me to be gone from them.

The job had been done and they had reluctantly paid the fees.

But there was to be one more fee to be paid before I was to leave.

I was too take with me a woman of the town as payment. But that was not all. I was commanded by the people that I was then to take her too the woods and after savouring my pleasures with her, that I was to take her life from her.

They had stated that I was to serve her with cruelty and pain. And then to cause her death in as vilest and sadistic a manner.

And so! I went too the house and knocked on the door.

At first there was no response. And so I hammered upon the door.

Eventually a sweet voice answered and I heard her call that she was coming.

But! I must start at the beginning of events. For if I do not then the truth will failed to be observed and a far greater amount of scorn and derision as well as intense hatred will be given too me to bare as my lot in life.

CHAPTER TWO

For some time creatures such as I had lived freely and in joy of life. Things had been good then. But that all changed and slowly the valleys and forests were changed.

And, as the changes came so did the evil of greed and corruption.

And we were forced to hide away in the caves of the mountains, the forests and even beneath the ground like frightened trolls.

But trolls we are not.

But we endured it all for there was still peace and contentment abounding for us.

But that did not last long! Soon we were discovered and we were captured and enslaved. And for some time the people would look and laugh as they mocked us.

But we bore it steadfastly. Believing in our hearts and knowing in our souls that freedom and redemption would be forthcoming, and that we would someday gain release. And it did. Though not in the way many of us thought possible.

There had been many natural disasters that befell the land from famine and pestilence through too floods and land-slides. Which these people found difficult to cope with. But they managed too all the same, as had we in our time.

But! Then came a terror that they found the weight of, almost too hard to bare.

When the land was lush and the crops were abundant all appeared to have turned out well. But that was not the case. For soon came the dawning of a new terror in the form of the over-whelming greed and avarice of the Overseer.

He was a brutish man who had an over-whelming appetite for wealth, especially other peoples.

His appetites did not rest there. For there were many reports of women of all ages as well as young children vanishing without trace. Farmlands were laid waste. And the homesteads were burnt too the ground.

He built himself a fortress of great size and complexity. There were many dark towers with high conical roofs.

Surrounding the fortress was a great moat that was as wide as it was deep.

There were two gates, one large gate with a great ramp at the front. At the rear was a small gate with a narrow entrance.

There were times when travellers would pass and be waylaid and forced to hand over their wares or suffer death. Which usually followed suit in virtually every case.

One traveller who was able to escape death did witness the ravishment and rape of his daughters and wife as well as his two maids before they and his three male servants were tortured too a slow agonizing death. Then their bodies were butchered and carried away too the fortress.

The traveller said that he believed that the bodies of his loved ones and servants were eaten within the fortress.

Eventually many stories of such horrors filtered throughout the village which had been slowly growing into a small town. That was until the arrival of the Overseer. Then all growth ceased.

There were some stories from people who had heard the screams of women and children within the fortress.

And one eyewitness account of two young women who after being violated a number of times by the Overseer's men, were taken and bound. One of the young women was then tied to a spit and roasted alive over a blazing fire. And after which some of the men proceeded to eat her. Whilst others took the second young woman and after violating her proceeded to bite her and to eat her alive. It was said that her screams of agony and horror seared through the forest and that all the creatures there-in did rush to escape the sounds that raked through their very bodies.

And that after that night of carnage and horror, no creature walked the path there. Nor did any bird sing. Even the night owls would fly around and away from there.

And so it was that I would find for a time solace there.

I had been captured by guards of the Overseer and brought too his fortress.

The men urged me forwards but were afraid to come too close to me as they had never seen a Dragon before.

So it was with a tinge of wonder and awe that they led me in to the presence of a very small, fat and exceedingly ugly little bald man.

He looked at me with as good a brave face as he could muster, but I could see the fear in him as was present in his men. I could smell the stench of their sweat mixed with the stink of burnt flesh.

I looked about me and saw young children and women of varying ages staring wildly at me.

Not knowing what horror was to be issued upon them.

A child screamed at me not eat it. But was silenced by a slashing blade.

The head lopped cleanly from its shoulders. The body was left to jerk and issue it's vitals through it's shoulders, accompanied by the screams of revulsion by the captive women and children.

'And what are you?' Shouted the little man not really expecting an answer.

I looked away from the dead young boy and stared straight at him.

'I am MORPHUS!'

'I ASKED WHAT YOU ARE! NOT WHO YOU ARE!' He bellowed.

I looked at him. I am a Dragon as you can see'.

And with that he looked fearfully at me and nodded and then I too was a prisoner as his men netted me and secured me.

'I have eaten children as well as women and some men! But I have never eaten a dragon before!' 'Take it away!'

And so I was removed to a dank cell.

After a few days which I received no food or water. I was removed from the cramped cell and taken back too his presence.

The Overseer sat on a large throne style seat, and at his feet was a beautiful young woman.

She looked at me and trembled in fear.

'You Dragon! You have been confined without food and water for some time now. For I knew not what to do with you.' He then looked at the woman.

'But I know now that I should not treat you as a prisoner, but as a guest. And so as I know you will be in need of sustenance and libation, I give too you this woman who as you can see is amply endowed. And she would make you a handsome meal.

I looked at her and saw the fear in her eyes and the trembling of her body as she prepared to meet death between my jaws.

I rose and moved forwards. I reached down and grasped her. I heard her screams as she beseeched me to spare her.

I looked at her. Then I turned my attention towards the little man on the huge throne.

'Why should I eat this human that you have offered me?'

'Because you are a Dragon and I command it!' Was his reply.

I looked at him and then placed the woman against my chest before I turned my head.

I then coughed and belched hot flame from my mouth which was followed by a searing, choking smoke as I covered the room.

I then drew a deep breath before expelling a fireball which struck the wall behind the overseer with such force that there appeared a great hole.

All about me were stunned and silent. Before I could turn my attentions towards the overseer, he had fled and his guards had followed suit leaving the captives to escape.

I then lowered the woman too the floor and pointed towards the hole, which was large enough for them all to get safely through. But it was still too small for me.

I urged them to leave and soon they got their wits about them and rushed from the great hall.

The woman looked back at me as I transcended to a smaller form.

There was a radiant smile on her face that over-whelmed me greatly. For never had I witnessed such beauty. And then it was gone as she vanished through the opening.

Suddenly I was aware that the guards had started streaming back into the hall, for they had witnessed my transcendence, and thus they evidently thought that as it had been a slow event, that they would have time to re-capture me.

This they found out was a big mistake. For it would take but no time at all to return too my normal size. But instead I remained as I was and just set up a nice choking smoke-screen which caused them a great deal of discomfort and also enabled my escape to be made.

Which I did with alacrity.

I left the hall via the hole I had created earlier and headed towards the moat. The crowd of panicking women and children had totally surprised the Gate guards and once they had been over-whelmed the women and children surged across the drawbridge.

When I approached the guards just threw their weapons aside and ran back into the fortress.

And so I found that as the gate and the drawbridge were deserted, that I had no rush to get across.

As I ambled away from the fortress I could here the panic laden shouts of the men as they fought to contain the fires I had started in the Great Hall of the Fortress.

I stopped and turned and I could see a faint glow from the fortress which was the light from the flames I had started and there was smoke issuing upwards in spiral.

But shortly the glow died as they put the flames out.

The young woman who had been offered too me came and tugged at my arm, insisting that we go from there.

I looked at her and saw the beauty in her face and the warmth in her eyes and I knew that I could never have anyone look at me such feeling ever again. For as suddenly the warmth vanished and she dropped my arm and left me.

I turned and went too the forest in the east where I had lived and where I longed to be.

As I entered the forest I heard the shouts of angry and violent men heading towards me. I was unarmed and so I chose to regain my natural form. And within seconds I was the large Red Dragon that they had witnessed before.

At my changing they all stopped and as I turned towards them they did back away, slowly at first and then with some haste. I think the fact that I issued forth a fireball in their direction may have helped them in coming to a decision to retreat as rapidly as they could.

I then turned away and continued to my home in a deep cave where all my belongings were, so that I could sleep.

CHAPTER THREE

The following morning I did arise to the sounds of birds singing and the warmth of the sun as well as the crispness of the fresh air.

I did move from my cave and so did I indulge and enjoy the full pleasures of flexing my wings as well as swishing my tail about me before I did stretch.

But my pleasures were short lived, for suddenly the birds did stop singing and all natural things were quiet, as the heavy sounds of marching boots and the clip-clopping of horses hooves did sound on the rocks and hard ground.

I turned my head and did see the Overseer sat astride a large black horse, regaled in fine black armour as was he.

I looked at the horde and thought that surely after they had seen what I could do too the stone walls of their Great Hall, that they would know that I could much worse to their weak flesh.

'YOU! DRAGON! I AM HERE TO TAKE YOU BACK BY ANY MEANS I HAVE TOO!' The Overseer did shout. And with that he lowered his lance, but not his visor.

Then from behind him rode four knights all in armour that bore a dull greyish tinge.

One by one did they take up post and upon his command did one spur his horse to lunge at me.

With but a flap of my great wings did I knock him from his horse. Then did I pick up his struggling form before I did set him down in the direction of the horde. He seemed to instinctively know which way to head and so he proceeded towards the Overseer.

As he reached the Overseer he was commanded to stop, which he did. Then the Overseer ordered the knight to remove his helmet.

As he did as commanded the Overseer nodded and as the helmet cleared the knights head, so was a bolt unleashed which struck him squarely in his head, rocking him backwards against a tree where he became impaled. And there he died, slowly.

That was a very simple message too the remaining three knights as well as too myself.

I could see that the knights knew that they had to either capture or kill me, or be killed either by me or by their own Master should they fail. This was re-enforce upon them when fires were lit and spits were put in place.

They evidently knew their Masters macabre ways well enough.

And so they decided between them that they would attack me as a group and not singularly.

And so I became forced to dispatch them all with my tail as well as with flame.

Upon seeing his remaining knights dispatched he called upon a fifth knight, who before advancing took a long spear and after thrusting it amongst the flames, did stand and wait as the tip became white hot.

Then did he advance too me at speed on his horse.

He did weave to and fro until he was in range and then he threw the spear, striking me in my right side.

The pain did seer through my body and such was my anger and grief that I gave vent and released upon him a tirade of fireballs that did strike him and did render him to ashes as his armour became molten and did pour along the furrows of the earth.

The heat did cause them all to retreat and so I did turn and go from them deep into the forest with the burning spear still embedded in my side.

Upon returning too my cave I did pull the spear from my side.

I knew that I could not repair my wound by my self and so I gathered to me my belongings and after changing my form I applied as best a dressing as I could find and set out towards the village.

As I neared the village I saw the young woman again and as she saw me she went to turn away, but when she noticed my difficulties, did she return too me and with her aid did I receive shelter at her home.

She was a strikingly beautiful and shapely young woman who did as it was apparent, lived alone.

She assisted me too a great couch and as I laid upon it, so did she search the building, eventually returning too me with a bowl of hot water, sponges, as well as dressings, bandages and a large brown pot containing some sort of balm.

She then tore at my clothing and after examining the wound she did bathe it and the warmth of the water did in deed cool the soreness. Then, did she apply the balm which was of such a soothing nature that I did almost succumb to sleep.

Once she had completed the application of the balm she did place upon me dressings and bandages which she secured before telling me to rest.

As I turned to rest on my left side I saw a look of fear cross her face.

'Fear not! I shall not change and become what I really am, nor will I mete unto you the horrors that may be traversing your silences of the mind!'

She looked quizzically at me and asked what I meant by the silences of the mind. So I replied that I meant her imagination. She appeared calmer and so did I sleep.

I know not for how long I slept, but it was a deep and much needed sleep I must admit.

She tended too me and fed me and not once, even though she was willing for me to do so, did I change back to my real self.

After a few more days, did I feel stronger and so I was preparing to go when there was a tumultuous row issuing from the streets which was pierced by the sounds of the young woman's screaming and begging voice.

As I listened I heard the crowd quieten as one voice rose to take control.

'You have been harbouring that creature! Have you not?' He shouted.

'He was hurt Father from the Overseer's men and so I tended too him. That is all!'

'Well we have business with him and so bring him too me! NOW GIRL!' he commanded.

So the young woman entered the house and came to me as I stood beside the fire.

She looked fearfully at me.

'Oh forgive me, but the townsfolk have come for you and I am so sorry.' She sobbed.

I turned and left the building through a door in the rear which led to a small courtyard. There did I change back too my real self, a great Red Dragon. I then left the courtyard and went into the square.

'WHOM IS SUCH THAT THEY DEMAND OF ME AN AUDIENCE!' Did I bellow as I showered flames and sparks skywards.

The crowd did turn as one.

Slowly and with excessive nervousness did the Churchman come forwards.

'I! I did request an audience of you Oh Great One.' He did stammer!

I looked down at him.

'And what do you require the outcome be of this audience?'

'My Lord and Mighty Dragon.' Did he begin. This caused me great amusement for he knew naught of how to address a Dragon. But then again I know not of how to address a Ruler. So we were quits.

'As you know,' he continued, 'we have been plagued for some time by the evil tyrant who has built upon us an impregnable fortress, and with such a place, does he wager terror upon us as well as any who so do pass.'

'And?' I asked as I began to grin.

'Well you see we had a meeting and it was decided that we should beseech upon you your mercies and seek for you to deliver us from this evil!'

'I see!' I replied. 'And for what will my payment be in this matter?'

The Churchman looked about the people and then back too me.

'Well my Lord! We shall of course give you whatsoever you require in food and drink as well as anything here that takes your fancy as well as a brand new suit of armour that our blacksmith has been preparing for you.

I looked down at him and nodded. 'Very well, this I will do for you!'

'There is one other little thing that is a favour of my own that I ask of you which would of course be part of the payment!'

'And what is that?' I asked.

'The woman who tended you is a witch and is causing myself some distress.

For she will not cease her actions nor will she take to husband any man of the town, and it was with her coming that shortly followed the Overseer and all our troubles. So! We all were hoping that you would see it in your path to remove her. And so doing could you do with her as you so wish, including the suggestion of the Overseer when she was a captive in the fortress!'

I looked at him and saw the weakness and smallness of him. But I must admit that I did find her beauty and kindness very becoming. But I also knew that as a Dragon, I was an ugly being too her as I was too all these people.

'So be it!' I replied and then I left them all.

I did stay with the young woman for a short while longer as I did visit the blacksmith as he furbished me with the armour and weapons for the work I had in mind.

I then bade her goodbye and went out to see what was ahead of me.

As I did near the fortress, so did I meet soldiers of the Overseer who did in turn attempt to waylay me, much too their ever increasing sorrow.

Upon reaching the fortress I could see that being in human form and in armour was not going to be a useful guise, and so I repaired too the forest where I did remove the armour before I did change back too my form as a Great Red Dragon.

Then, did I leave the forest and go too the fortress. As I neared the dark wet moat that surrounded the fortress I did see men running in an almost haphazard way about the fortifications, shouting and gesticulating wildly and trying to convey their urgencies too one another by at times pointing at me.

I watched and listened for a while and then sat and rested, keeping an ever watchful eye upon the fortress.

After a day of resting, did I eat of the provisions I had with me. Then I arose and went too the large gate house. I looked at it for a while and then turned and retreated back too the forest, accompanied by the sounds of cheering as the men on the parapets did think that I had seen my failure and my cowardice.

For two days did I remain in the forest, watching and listening.

And for all of those two days, did the drawbridge not lower. But, on the third day the bridge did lower and a group of knights in tarnished armour did nervously emerge.

I remained silent and just lay still as I watched them.

They did appear to be building a camp a few yards ahead of the fortress as though they were to be the advanced warning party.

So I just waited until night came and then I changed into my human form and after donning my armour, which the blacksmith had been able to create in a very light and durable way, I fastened my weapons too my waist of a broad sword as well as a dagger.

I then left the shadows of the forest and travelled towards the rear of the fortress. There I saw encamped about five hundred paces was a second encampment. I circled them and after much stealth did I come upon the rear door which had a small raising gate bridge, which was in the lowered position. I doubted very strongly that the men from either encampment, upon sighting me as the Dragon would have managed to get back across the bridges before they were fully raised. So they were to be sacrificed in a delaying tactic. For I am certain that the Overseer believed fully that upon my meeting with them I would naturally dispose of them all, with possibly some injury too my self, and that I would then settle down for a nice meal of dead human flesh.

I smiled into the visor of my helmet as I neared the small bridge. I then crossed and reached the wooden door. I turned the handle on the door and pushed at it. Slowly at first it did open. I did not pursue opening it fully, but sufficient for me to gain entrance.

Once inside I did close and lock the door.

I then stopped and listened to voices.

Voices of very nervous sounding men who knew not their fate.

I then found a room near the scarred Great Hall. I crept in to it and hid for a while. I listened too the conversations of the men, which suddenly rang silent as the Overseer entered the Great Hall.

I knew that I could not do anything against the number of men in the fortress in my present form, and so I disrobed from my armour and placed it all quietly in a sac that I had been carrying on my back.

Then I started the change. But this time I commenced at a slow rate so that I could give a continual pressure too the room I was in so that I would force the walls to explode and thus would I cause great confusion, which I would use to my advantage.

And so as I grew so did my plan go into place, until the whole building shook as the walls of the room I was in exploded. Then did I enter the room. I did not waste time with searching for the Overseer, for I could see him sitting on his throne in all his false regal splendour.

And so, to amend any oversight I had had on our first encounter there

I did not display the correct amount of courtesy, did I issue forth a rapid succession of fireballs that did seer the building walls. All the fancy drapes did burst into flames as fixtures melted along with empty and full suits of armour which were accompanied by screams of agony and pain.

I did not stop until I rendered the fortress to rubble. The Overseer sat slumped on his throne a spear embedded in his chest. His face looking skywards with a stare of total disbelief.

I then turned and saw the remaining men running as fast as their cumbersome armour would allow them.

I then turned my attention to destroying as much of the fortress as I could before I too left the area.

I made my way back too the town, stopping long enough to change into human form and to again don the armour.

And then as it was late, did I take repose beside the river at the towns edge.

And so I rested as the waters of the river wound steadily by, sweeping all that fell too it's surface along with it in an urgency that it alone knows.

I sat by it's side watching as the World unfurled it's knowledge too me in silence. And in silence I absorbed and learnt.

But the weight of life and memories laid heavy upon me and my soul cried out in anguish and pain as I took repose. But there is no rest or peace for such as I.

No! There can only be pain, anguish and suffering. For time and life is of such a magnitude of indifference to such as I that my ignominy is of such little consequence that naught of attentions by passers-by are conveyed towards me.

My existence is but a whim of their imaginations that are but fleeting glimpses into their being. And soon they are gone and I remain in silent repose.

Steadily the wind does rise as the clouds ramble in too cover the dwindling blue sky in all their majesty as the time rolls away and slowly day becomes night.

The clouds take command and the Moon in rising struggles vainly too cast the afterglow of the passing sun onto the face of the Earth.

And still I remain.

For there is naught for me to energize over. All is at peace and such as I are not called upon to wage battle for others.

And so it is with a sadness that I rest my head and think of my existence upon this Earth. And I recall the joy at encountering people who beseeched such as I to come too them, only for me to feel the horrors of their revulsion and scorn that was eventually heaped upon such liken too myself.

And so I sit here in silence as I listen too the continuing chatter of the river as it wends away from me.

I remain and wait for my last breath and dream of the peace that is never to be mine.

I wait for the Angel of Death to take my last breath away with naught but a scant look back at my slumped body. And for me to become chilled by the Angels scorn towards me.

But throughout the night there is no sign of my death.

And so I must remain too serve all who bid me too do their will.

And in turn for me to be in receipt of their abuse and revulsion at the sight of my existence.

Oh that I could be given release. That I may stay by the river and dream and never have to fight again.

But that will never be.

Slowly the dark clouds give way too greyness as the sun rises, enshrouded by the morning cloudy sky.

I listened too the river, but all was still around.

I looked and saw people moving towards me. At first I saw their stiffening as they espied my prone figure.

Steadily, as before they cross away from me. Averting from me are their gazes, as they fuss with one-another in an effort to ignore me.

To obliterate me from their sight and mind.

So! Slowly as the morning begins I slowly rise. I gather my belongings before I arrange my weapons. The people near me rush to depart from me.

Slowly but steadily there comes the Churchman.

I overt my eyes, for I feel that am unworthy to look upon him. He falters in his step as he nears me.

For a moment his gaze meets mine as he looks up at my face. But there was nothing he could see as my helmet and visor covered my head and face.

Suddenly there was a darkening of his face as he looked at my armoured body.

And the realization that he was standing in front of something that he had no desire to be near over-took him with alacrity and he suddenly jerked away from me and his step quickened as he rushed to away from my being.

Slowly a smile crept across my mouth as I watched him join the scurrying throng, who seemed to be so pre-occupied with escaping the vicinity of my being.

I then turned and steadily walked into the town.

I saw people rush away and I heard doors crashing shut as I neared them.

From all the windows I saw peering faces. Faces full of hatred and fear.

Faces of people who had earlier beckoned me too them with open arms. But who now wished for nothing more than for me to be gone from them.

The job had been done and they had reluctantly paid the fees.

But there was to be one more fee to be paid before I was to leave.

I was too take with me a woman of the town as payment. But that was not all.

I was commanded by the people that I was then to take her too the woods and after savouring my pleasures with her, that I was to take her life from her.

They had stated that I was to serve her with cruelty and pain. And then to cause her death in as vilest and sadistic a manner.

And so! I went too the house and knocked on the door.

At first there was no response. And so I hammered upon the door.

Eventually a sweet voice answered and I heard her call that she was coming.

As she opened the door there came the crowd with the Churchman at their head.

'TAKE HER! TAKE HER!' He shouted. 'SHE IS YOUR PRIZE TO DO WITH AS YOU SO DESIRE BEFORE HER DEATH!

I turned my head to him and wished to breath fire over them and to rend them to cinders.

But I had given my word that I would take her away.

'Come with me!' I did command of her.

She looked fearfully at me but did do as commanded.

The crowd did accompany us too the edge of the town jeering at her all the way.

I led her too the river and then beyond into the forest and too my cave.

'What will you do with me now my Lord?'

'Why? What will you have me do with you?' I asked.

She then sank too her knees and pleaded forgiveness and mercy and to be spared, in the same way that she had when she had been offered too me by the late Overseer.

Harm too her I could not bring to do, and so I released her.

But go, she did not and we have remained together ever-since, for without knowing it I had saved and released a female Dragon of such beauty and magnitude that I am over-whelmed and we are now 'Life Partners' through all eternity.

THE DRAGON AND THE MINERS

by
Richard Glyndwr Evans

The skies were reddened by the belching flames from the furnaces as the molten metals were poured and cast from the great coal-fired steel works in the valleys.

The men in the foundries toiled ceaselessly to create the forms that the people in the big cities and the industries needed.

And, as these men worked in the intense heat they created, and the people of the villages, towns and cities went about their daily lives, below ground a hidden band of men who toiled in the oppressive heat and darkness.

Facing the dangers of cave-ins, flooding as well as gassing and fire. Not to mention injuries and even death from mechanical accidents.

And it was on one of these nights that events in one colliery changed and not for the better.

The men at the coalface were toiling as usual to bring too the surface the much-needed coal that would be burned in the homes; foundries and industries as well as the steam engines and steam powered ships. But unlike all those who worked above, these men were ever vigilant for the different sounds and actions of the face as well as the gallery ceiling and floor. As a subsidence could easily spell disaster which would probably end in death for at least some of the men if not all.

And so it was with a sudden shout of alarm that a miner shouted out that he had heard a sound like a deep rumble.

All the men downed tools and as silence reigned throughout the gallery, they listened intently. Suddenly there was too all of them the clear deep sound of a rumbling which was shortly followed by the sound of running water.

The men looked about them and then they saw that running from the ceiling too the floor was a steady stream of water.

They watched the water and saw that it was coming in faster than it could empty.

The Charge-hand rushed back too the pumps and set them working. Then the men just watched, as the water seemed to drop in level as the pumps engaged.

But the level dropped only a small amount before it started to rise until all the men knew that the pumps would not be able to hold and compete against the flow of, by now, cascading water.

And so they turned to escape back too the tower to get too the lifts and freedom.

But that was not to happen. For suddenly there was an almighty great crack as the timbers started to break under the strain.

Now it was at this time that a great slumbering red dragon was aroused from his sleep as the noise of the water and the earth as well as the raising voices of the miners reached him.

The dragon had not seen a human being for at least five hundred years and so was startled to hear them so closely.

He listened at the sounds of nature, as he steadily became aware of the cries of the men, as the realization that death would take them eventually away from their loved one's topside!

The dragon decided that he should go too them. So with great lumbering movements he stretched himself before slowly turning about to face the direction of the voices, which had now seemed to change from a panic too that of a soft singing voice which was now resigned too the events of the situation.

The Dragon used his mighty talons as he powerfully dug his way through too the gallery. And as he neared the men he heard their voices. Voices he had not heard in centuries.

They were the voices of Welsh Pitmen who were singing their last praises to the Lord God!

Suddenly all the voices stopped as the thunderous rumbling of the earth increased. And as one they all turned their heads too the coalface and saw the appearance of an Angel in shimmering white.

As the Angel appeared, so did the great dragon. The men heard the sound of him as they felt his great hot breath fall upon them. And as they looked from the Angel towards the Dragon, he did see the fear in their eyes.

And he knew that though they had prepared for death, they now felt a fear far greater. A fear of being shown no mercy in any form. And that here was the true implement of their deaths. And that they would suffer greatly at the hands of this apparition that stood before them breathing flames and snorting black smoke.

Would they be burnt to death. Or would the dragon just rip them limb from limb for its pleasure. Or would it just stand there and watch as one by one they all succumbed and then for it to pounce upon them and desecrate their lifeless bodies. All these thoughts and more went through their minds.

Suddenly the dragon moved forwards as the Angel faltered from its moving forwards, which the miners had not detected.

For if, the Angel had touched any of them, then death would have followed swiftly. But the Angel knew better than to argue with the Great Red Dragon. For though the miners knew not about the Dragon, the Angel knew that he was a Sentinel of God's and he was the overseer for God of the Earth and all Creation.

And so the Angel retired too the recesses of the gallery as the Dragon spread his great wings and with an ear-shattering roar took up a position which shielded the miners from the roof as it started to crumble upon them.

'Go! Go!' He roared.

'Flee too the surface!'

The miners were stunned, but were soon in motion as one man they headed for the tower and the lifts too the surface and life.

The men emerged at the surface and all was joy and they as well as their families and friends had great relief as the sunlight of the early morning fell upon them through the cloudy haze. And the air had never felt so sweet.

For a while confusion reigned in part due too the great relief that everyone felt.

Then came the matter of relating what had happened.

And as the men related all that had happened a deep hush fell upon the pit head as the men told of the appearance, firstly of the Angel and then of the great red creature that stood and took the great weight of the gallery roof, and who had ordered them to make their escape.

Suddenly there was a very deep but loud rumble as the ground shifted. And all the people rushed to get away from the area.

Suddenly a little girl looked up at one of the miners and asked him about the Dragon?

'Dragon! Dragon! Well I suppose what ever it was will have died now. For child! Nothing could live down there after the ground has given away. Which it has by now no doubt done'.

'But should we not try to see and help him if he is still alive'? She asked.

For a short while everyone looked around at each other and then at the girl.

No one said a word for they felt that they could not chastise her. And what if it was still alive and now needed their help.

And so! Without further ado, they started to organize themselves and to sort out the equipment that they would need. If not to rescue the Dragon, to at least retrieve his body.

And so the men prepared to return too the bowels of the ground.

As they were doing this the Dragon stood his ground and though he knew his strength was slowly being sapped away from him as the water reached the level of his belly. He braced himself.

The Angel had remained and there was a gentle smile on the Angels face as he watched over the Dragon.

'Get thee away Angel! You have lost the souls of innocent men this time!' Roared the Dragon.

'That is true,' replied the Angel. 'But I will now have your soul to take too the Lord! You have served as the Sentinel for long enough and now I think you will return with me!'

'And what is there for me, but oblivion upon my return.'

'That is so Dragon, for your time is ended! Humans do not believe in you anymore except for their stories of times gone by.'

At this the Dragon gave out one great roar as flame spewed forth from his mouth accompanied by great billows of black smoke from his flared nostrils.

The Angel again smiled as he watched the Dragons strength begin to ebb.

But the Angels smile was short lived for a fraction of time as he heard the sounds of the miners returning.

But then his smile returned.

'Well Dragon! If the water or the weight does not pass you into my hands, then the returning men will surely kill you in their fear of you as you stand powerless and defenceless.

The Dragon just looked at the Angel and did not blink as the men eased forwards carrying tools and pipes as well as devices to prop and support the ceiling.

Slowly at first the Dragon felt the weight ease and the strain on his mighty back ease.

Then he heard the cries of the men as the success of their labours was realized, and the face was saved along with the life of the Great Red Dragon. Then the men moved aside as the Angel turned away from them with their joyful cries ringing in his ears as the Great Red Dragon slowly turned away.

The men cheered and led the Dragon from the gloom of the tunnelled ground to the surface.

And! As they all emerged into the sunlight all assembled cheered and applauded at the sight of the Great Red Dragon.

And he marvelled that none of the people attempted to run away from him.

But his heart was touched as the little girl walked up to him and smiled as she looked up into his tired eyes.

So the Great Dragon lowered his head and then he growled softly as she stroked him before climbing onto his powerful and broad back.

And from that time on, the Great Red Dragon watched over the villagers and the miners, and he found harmony and love and most of peace, as he found that he no longer had to reside in the Silences of the Mind. But could live with and amongst humans. And that the kindness they bestowed upon him was magnificent.

There were times when he would hear the people laughing about his existence too strangers and that they would impress upon the strangers that the stories were only tales of myth, and the fanciful babblings of fools!

And so the Great Red Dragon lived, and still lives in peace and harmony. And still does he do the bidding of God!

And that is one of the reasons why we have a Red Dragon on the Flag of Cymru!

A TIME TO REMEMBER

by
Richard Glyndwr Evans

The sun shone down warmly upon the land. The birds did fly over head in lazy swooping motions as they rode the warmed air as it rose to the heights.

There was a light breeze though nothing to trouble either the soaring birds nor the people and animals on the ground.

The grass was lush and the fields full of ripening harvest that would soon be gleaned by the farmers and their workers.

Shopkeepers sold their wares to the ladies and gentlemen of the town. And the young children played in the park whilst the older children went about their studies in the schools.

Along with this did stand a policeman who did watch the traffic as it passed him by. Occasionally he would nod to a pedestrian as they approached him.

There was even one time when he became involved in a social chitchat with a passer-by who he knew.

And as all appeared so calm and peaceful, deep in the forest on the edge of the town, there did approach a dark cave, a creature all dressed in black.

A dark forbidding creature of great height, walked as a man, who did pay not the slightest jot of attention to his surroundings. He strode forwards with purpose in every step.

He neither looked left nor right, just straight-ahead. People who walked the path he was on would stand aside as he approached them. He neither saw nor paid any attention of them.

To all who saw him, they were of the same state of mind that he was oblivious to them. The men looked upon him in fear. The women looked in awe of him. But the children, they looked and smiled at him. And there were times when a smile would start to appear. But as quickly as it appeared, so did it vanish.

Eventually the creature did arrive at his destination. It was then that he did stop and look around him.

Slowly did he survey his surroundings before he did recommence walking. He crossed from the path to the lush green grass. It was noted by a young woman to her beau, that as the creature did step onto the grass that he left no footprint.

They looked on as the tall creature continued to stride unerringly towards the cavernous mouth of a dark cave.

There was nothing but silence as he neared the cave. No birds sang nor flew near it, no animals roamed or rested near the cave, though moments before there had been.

Without the slightest hesitation the tall dark creature did enter the cave mouth. He then stopped. And before the eyes of those who watched, did he so change and become the blackest of black Dragons to be ever seen.

He turned and looked at the people amassing on the path and they saw his eyes burn brightly with a redness that mesmerized them all.

He then raised his gigantic black wings before he raised his head and spewed forth flame and smoke.

Then did his voice growl forth as he summoned the Great Red Dragon who dwelt within the cave.

'Come! Come unto me Morphus! I command you!' Did the Great Black Dragon call.

At first there was just the diminishing echo of his powerful voice, which was then followed by cold silence that appeared to last for ages to the watching and gathering crowd.

Eventually there did emanate from within a deep and heavy rumble. The crowd all gasped loudly as the Great Black Dragon did back from the mouth of the cave into the sunlight where he did take post with his great black wings raised.

Slowly the rumbling sound did get louder and deeper as the Great Red Dragon did near from within the mouth to the cave.

As the Great Red Dragon did enter into the sunlight, so did the crowd gasp with awe as they saw for the very first time this magnificent Dragon in his entire splendour.

'WHO SO CALLS ME FROM MY REST?' Did he bellow.

'I call unto and upon you Draig Morphus!' was the reply.

'And who be you to raise me to this world?' asked Morphus.

'I, who am known as Draig Angau call upon you Draig Morphus. For Time is Time!

The two dragons looked to each other for a few moments. And the gathering crowd did look on in wonder and awe. For they did expect that soon, a great and bloody battle would ensue between these two mystical and mighty creatures.

'Is the black one making a challenge?' asked a young woman.

'My money is on the Red Dragon,' said one man.

'Shall we have a wager?' asked another.

But before they could speak further the two dragons did turn towards the crowd before stepping forth.

As they neared the crowd it did start to disperse and leave a pathway open for the two mighty creatures to walk down unhindered.

For once did the great black dragon look about him.

'And you care for these humans?' He asked of Morphus.

'I do!' Was the reply.

They then continued in silence until they reached a large grassy clearing.

Here they did stop and rest and talk a while with the crowd maintaining a healthy distance from them.

Then without any further ado, both mighty creatures did rise into the air on their great wings and so they did spiral ever upwards until the crowd could not see them as they became hidden by clouds.

They did fly ever upwards until they were no longer of this world but had travelled through the Portals of Heaven, where they did see and meet others of their kind as well as Angels and Messengers.

CHAPTER TWO.

Eventually did they arrive at a massive and fine set of golden gates. At these gates did stand an Angel and with him did stand two great red dragons. One either side of the gates.

'This is as far as I am allowed Draig Morphus. You must now continue in the Angels Company.' And with that Draig Angau, the Great Black Dragon did turn away from Morphus.

'Come with me,' said the Angel. And without any hesitation did the Angel so turn and lead the way through the gates, which appeared to open by their own will.

The Angel did seem to glide along the path and though he seemed to be keeping pace with Morphus, at no time did he attend Morphus' side. Nor did he speak one word more than he had at the gate.

Eventually they did near a gigantic structure that defies all human descriptions, for none could allude clearly and fully to its monumental grandness, for no language born has enough words to describe what Morphus did behold with his green eyes.

The Angel then turned to Morphus and pointed to the ground.

'You are not permitted to enter above that step. Be advised to keep your station dragon!' He then left, leaving Morphus to await his fate.

Now unlike humans, Dragons do not ponder their fate and the myriad possibilities of its execution. For they ask for nothing and expect nothing. No promises have made been to Dragons and so no promises can be broken.

And so did Draig Morphus stand and wait.

For four days did he stand and wait. Not once did he sit nor lie. Nor did he slumber as he waited.

Eventually on the fifth day did another Angel approach him.

She smiled at him and bade him ascend the steps.

'I am not permitted beyond this point Angel', did Morphus state.

'Whys is that so?' She asked of him.

'I know not, other than I have been told by the Angel who brought me hither from the Golden Gates.'

The Angel smiled and told Morphus that his Time was Time and that his Master would speak with him.

For once in all his long life Morphus was visibly shocked and found that he could not move.

He just stood and looked at the Angel. Eventually he regained his composure and as he stepped forwards he did close his wings tightly. He noted that this Angel did walk alongside him and that she continued to smile at him.

'You fear nothing Dragon?' She did ask of him.

'There is nothing to fear other than failure in doing my Masters bidding!' Morphus replied.

Eventually they arrived at the Great Hall where the Angel did ask Morphus to wait a while as he would soon be called.

As he stood there, he did witness many comings and goings of different people. Some looking very smug when they went in, though most did not appear to be so smug when they came back past him.

Others looked glum, and for some the gloom seemed to be increased. There was a whole gamut of expressions and emotions on display that Morphus lost track of them all.

Eventually he was summoned to a great and glittering hall where he found he was alone.

Suddenly a powerful voice called to him.

'DRAIG MORPHUS! YOU WHO HAVE BEEN SUMMONED BEFORE ME! IT IS YOUR TIME OF TIME!'

Morphus could not tell where the voice came from nor did he think about it. For it was not his place to know, and he accepted that.

'YOU WHO ATTEND ME ARE TO LOOK BACK AND REMEMBER AND TO RECITE TO ME ALL THAT YOUR LIFE IS AND WHAT IT IS WORTH!' Continued the voice.

Morphus stared fixedly at the ground.

Then slowly did he raise his head and so did face the voice and countenance of his Master. He did not falter his gaze nor did he stare in neither defiance nor superiority. For he had never had any such feelings.

'I know not where to begin Master.'

'RELATE TO ME ALL YOU'RE EXPERIENCES AND THOSE THINGS I GAVE YOU CALLED EMOTIONS!'

And so Morphus did start to relate all that he had witnessed and done.

Of all his feelings and emotions.

And after many days his Master did stand and walk to him.

'MORPHUS, YOU HAVE TOLD ME ALL THAT I KNOW AND I KNOW ALL AS I AM YOUR MASTER'. 'AND YOU TELL ME SOMETHING THAT YOUR WORDS DO NOT TELL ME! THAT THOUGH YOU HAVE SUFFERED THE FEAR OF HUMANS, AND YET YOU SO DO LOVE THEM THAT YOU BEG FOR OBLIVION SO THAT THEY MAY LIVE

IN PEACE, HARMONY AND JOY AS WELL AS ETERNAL LOVE.' 'YOU WOULD CEDE TO ME YOUR EXISTENCE FOR ALL OF THIS TO BE GRANTED UNTO THEM?'

Morphus looked to the ground. 'Yes my Master, that and all that you would demand of me to achieve that for them and you.

The Master did then turn aside and beckoned to him anther Angel. He instructed the Angel to return Morphus to the Golden Gates where Morphus was to await the coming of Draig Angau.

This was done and Morphus was told to stand and wait for the Death Dragon, Draig Angau.

For two weeks did Morphus await the arrival of Draig Angau.

Eventually the Great Black Dragon appeared at the Golden Gates with three other Dragons, one green, one yellow and one white.

He looked at Morphus. 'I will escort back to your cave and you will await my return to you'.

And with that he returned Morphus at dead of night to his cave, before he departed he afforded Morphus with one last instruction. That Morphus was not to leave his cave. Not even for food nor water.

And so Morphus did remain an unchained prisoner in his own cave. No food nor water did pass his lips.

Eventually months passed and as he hungered and thirst did rise to him so did he become weaker.

And as he weakened so did he receive a visitor in the form of an Angel.

'I know you Dragon, oh yes I do!' 'You are of he who did stop me taking the miners souls these many past years. And unfortunately they did stop me from taking him. But revenge I shall have. For it is you will be passed to me!' And so saying the Angel did vanish as quickly as he had appeared.

CHAPTER THREE

Eventually did Morphus hear the strong voice of Draig Angau at the cave entrance summoning him to attend.

And so with great difficulty did Morphus raise himself to his feet. Where upon he stumbled forwards to the hailing voice and the light.

Slowly did Morphus emerge from the gloom of the cave unto the daylight.

'Look you upon the ground and the trees, listen to the birds and the animals. bathe in the sunlight this last time Dragon. For the Master has made his decision'.

'And what decision has my Master cast for me?'

'That you who have protected these people and who have also begged and pleaded with him to send you to Oblivion so that they may Live has been this day granted.'

'This day you will come with me and you will grasp Oblivion and it shall consume you.'

Then the Great Black Dragon did rise aloft in the air above Morphus.

Morphus summoned all his strength and slowly did ascend to the skies.

Then he looked down and saw the crowds all gazing up at him. Then he saw that where his cave had been, there was naught but a huge chasm of swirling mist.

'YOU ARE COMMANDED BY THE MASTER TO DIVE AND ENTER THE OBLIVION. TO BE FORGOTTEN BY ALL. TO BE CONSIGNED TO A NON EXISTENCE FOR ALL TIME AND BEYOND!' 'GO NOW!' growled loudly the Great Black Dragon

And so did Morphus circle three times before he raised his head skywards and with one last gasp did thank his Master, before he furled his wings and plummeted towards the Chasm of Oblivion.

As he fell towards his destiny, he could hear the crowd gasping. None cheered nor laughed. But many cried and wailed and cried to God to save Morphus from his fate.

But all appeared to be of no avail as he did plummet towards Oblivion.

Suddenly two voices cried out as one, 'TAKE ME!'

The crowd looked as a little boy and a little girl from different ends of the crowd screamed out.

And as they did the heavens thundered and lightening flashed and the Great Black Dragon did land and call them to him.

As he did this Morphus found himself cradled above the chasm, though not free of it?

The Great Black Dragon looked down at the children.

'Do you know who and what I am?' He asked of them gently.

They looked and stared at him as they shook their heads in unison.

'My name is Draig Angau which means Death Dragon. And I come to collect the souls of all Dragons to take them to where they are commanded to be by our Master.'

The little boy and girl looked at him with unflinching eyes.

'And are you taking the Dragon to where he has been commanded to go?' They asked.

'No! I am sending him to where he said he would willingly go for you all to live in Love, Joy, Harmony and Peace.'

'So he is giving his life for us?' Asked a young man who stood behind the children.

'Yes! He is giving his life for you!' Replied the Great Black Dragon.

'But that is not right.' Said the young man.

And then the crowd started to come alive and they too expressed their desire for the Great Red Dragon to live.

Suddenly a silence pervaded as a voice silenced them all.

'SILENCE YE ALL! WOULD YOU ALL DEFY MY WILL FOR THE SAKE OF A DRAGON? WOULD YOU ALL INCUR MY WRATH FOR THIS?'

'YES WE WOULD DO ALL THAT AND MUCH MORE!' They did reply as in one voice.

Suddenly Morphus found himself no longer being cradled above the chasm, but being lowered to the ground amidst the crowd.

'KNOW YOU THIS MORPHUS!' said Draig Angau. 'THE MASTER HAS SEEN WHAT YOU ARE AND WHAT YOU HAVE DONE AND HE IS WELL PLEASED WITH YOU. LIVE YOUR LIFE AMONGST THESE PEOPLE AND PROTECT THEM AS YOU ALWAYS HAVE AND LOVE THEM AS YOU ALWAYS WILL. YOUR PRAYERS HAVE BEEN ACCEPTED AND REALIZED, IN THE MASTERS NAME AMEN!'

And with that the skies brightened and the Great Black Dragon did rise into the heavens, to vanish into the clouds and thence to return to his home in Eternity.

REASON TO BELIEVE IN

by
Richard Glyndwr Evans

Every day of each year that passed had been totally the same, people went to work, by bus, car, train, bike and foot. And at the end of their work they went home the same way.

Some would have a good day at work, and others would not. And some would have an exceptional day which brought to them great joy.

And then they would return to their homes at the end of the working day.

Some would go to a bar for a drink before catching their bus or train home.

Others would just sit in their cars and chat with their friends as they got stuck in a traffic jam, whilst others would listen to the radio or a tape or a cd playing. And others would get irate at the same old situation that they found themselves in day in and day out.

Now at one point in the year there always came the inevitable need to go shopping. This was not shopping for food stuffs. Oh no! This was shopping for toys and other presents. For it was that time when humans would give cards and gifts to their loved one's as well as their friends and work colleagues.

It was that time when adult's would tell their children about Santa Clause and Christmas, and then some would also take their children to the local store and let them see Santa in his Grotto attended by his Elf's who all looked like young girls. None were real elves. And in fact when the children left and the Grotto closed, Santa would take off his fake white beard and wig and then change from his bright red suit and black boots and change into his normal day clothes, then he too goes his way from the store, as do all the others who work at portraying Santa.

And sometimes if the shoppers and children are lucky they witness the snow falling about them.

Though others were not that fortunate to see the snow as they live in places where the snow never falls.

But they still would have a good and merry time.

Every year the parents would take their youngest children to the stores to see 'Santa in his Grotto'. But slowly as the children grew up they became less and less into wanting to go to see Santa and they would just tell their Mum's and Dad's what they wanted for Christmas.

And steadily the stores began to advertise Christmas toys in the April of each year.

Now as it came to pass the Dragon had witnessed the changes over the years, and not only in the loss of belief in Santa, but in the way that everything was becoming more of a commercial event. The people had also seemed to loose the point of Christmas.

And so it continued, year after year.

One day when the snows laid deep, crisp and even in the park, a lone stooped figure of some portly proportions, did make his way along the whitened paths until he passed the trees and a small group of children playing in the snow. He stopped and looked to his left and saw more children riding sledges down the steep bank of snow covered ground. He could hear their yells and screams as they played.

He heard the calls from their Mothers and Fathers to 'be careful'.

He stood for a while and watched them.

As he stood there, he became aware of a little girl standing looking up at him.

"Who are you?" she asked.

"No one special". Was his sad reply, as he lowered his head against the wind as he turned away from the girl.

He walked onwards along the path, passing many people who did not give him a second glance.

None of them saw the redness of his cape nor his bright red tunic.

None saw the shininess of his highly polished black boots.

None marvelled at his white hair that peaked from beneath his bright red bonnet.

None saw his white beard and moustache, be speckled with the snow that was caught in it.

Eventually he came to the fencing that surrounded a high clump of rocks which stood alone from everything else.

He walked along the fencing until he saw the gaping blackness of the cave mouth.

He listened but only heard the sounds of merrymaking nearby.

He saw that some children did play near to the cave mouth. But none ventured in. But to his stare, they did not seem a-feared of the cave, nor of what was within. They were to busy playing and enjoying the winter snows.

He opened the kiss-gate and walked steadily towards the cave-mouth.

The children playing near the cave mouth stopped as he neared them and stared at him as he walked into the cave.

The man could hear the questioning sounds of the children behind him as well as the heavy breathing of the creature within whom he sought.

Suddenly he halted as he heard the lumbering movement from within as the great creature stirred.

"Who be thou, who so does disturb me in my time", roared the creatures powerful voice which was soon followed by billowing smoke and a heat that would sear the skin from a man in seconds.

"It is I who would disturb you Dragon! For I will have words with you!" Replied the Man of Red.

He stood still as he heard the sounds of the great dragon as it did move towards him.

"What words wouldst thou have of me?"

The man looked incredulously at the great dragon who stood in all it's glorious magnificence before him.

He knew that this was not a creature to be trifled with, nor was it a creature who would be impressed by him nor what he stood for.

"Do you know who I am", asked the man?

"That I do!" Replied the Dragon. "And what would you have of me?"

CHAPTER TWO

The man looked at the Dragon and then sat on a nearby rock.

"I wish to know why we both stay and do not go away as people would wish us to?"

"And do they wish this of us?" Asked the Dragon.

"I fear it is so for they do not seem to care anymore!"

"Why doest thou sayest this?" Asked the Dragon.

"I look at this world and marvel how it is that everything has a price and that everything is marketable, and yet what the real meaning of my existence is totally forgotten."

The dragon looked at the man and then sat and let great billows of smoke rise from his slightly flared nostrils.

"You who have been around as long as man has known of you now question as to your worth, their worth or both?"

I question that and so much more. I do not know why I continue. For Christmas is such a short time and all that is good is so shortly forgotten."

The dragon looked directly at the man then out through the cave mouth where he saw the children playing.

"Why do you seek answers and confirmations from me," the Dragon asked?

"What answers can I give unto you that will ease your mind and set you forwards?"

The man looked at the dragon in despair.

"I tell you this old man. That every day at least one child is born to this world and that child grows up knowing of you and the goodness that is you. Yes they may forget as time passes and as they grow up in this world. But, every year comes the time when they have no choice to remember and to think. And in time they meet and marry and they in their turn have children. And they do tell them stories of Santa Clause and they do watch films of the stories of you, and they do decorate their houses and have great joy. Each home you enter is decorated with splendour and each home you enter holds a welcoming for you!"

The man nodded his agreement.

The Dragon looked at him.

"But! What do you see of them towards my kind? What joy do they give unto my kind when we roamed freely?"

The man looked down in sadness.

"Yes! Look away from me. For I am the epitome of ugliness and cruelty. I am nothing more than a diabolical creature that does deserve nothing more than their contempt and distrust!"

"Yes! I have seen and heard that." whispered the man.

"You! You have a family to return to. But I! I who had my Morphusa, I am now alone. And I must remain so until my Time is Time.

"But were you not summoned to the Great One? And did you not give evidence to Him of the goodness you found in these people?"

The Dragon looked at the man and smiled.

"Yes I did. I did relate all my experiences with them and how many that had been kind to me. That I had no reason to forsake one of them. That in my eyes, they were all worthwhile."

CHAPTER THREE

The man looked at the dragon before speaking.
"But was it not a man who did slay your Morphusa?" asked the man.
The dragon did look wistfully at the man.
"No! He did not slay her. He took her away from me and imprisoned her. But she was rescued and dwells now with others of my kind in the Masters Garden."
"But you are alone and confined to this cave!"
"You believe that then?"
"Well it is obvious is it not? For you are known to hardly ever venture from this cave and it is believed that you are forced to forage for food by night." replied the man.
"I see!" smiled the dragon.
"Then come with me and watch." And with that the dragon moved passed the still seated man of red.
The Dragon moved towards the mouth of the cave and did not hesitate to exit the cave.
And as he did so the man heard the screams and cries. And he did think, that the dragon had indeed frightened the children away, for he was a fearsome sight to behold.
And so he jumped up and rushed from the cave. But the sight that did greet his tired eyes was so stunning that he found himself on his knees in the deep snow and staring wildly as

he saw the children climbing all over the dragon. Even adults came up and stroked him and talked with him. And he saw the dragon answer them in deep whispers.

He saw children sitting on his neck and stoking him.

He saw one little girl sitting between his ears and stroking his comb.

He was amazed at the joy that was given to the dragon. He saw one old lady come to the dragon and offer him food. And in his turn the dragon did lower his left wing and did enshroud the woman to warm her. Others sheltered under his out-stretched right wing from the snow.

The man watched amazed as some children did use the dragons long red tail as a slide.

He was amazed as they all played with glee.

And how the children did laugh when they threw snowballs at the dragon only to see them melted by his hot breath before they could hit him.

He watched as they cheered and laughed when the dragon would let the occasional snowball hit him.

He was suddenly stunned when a fusillade of snowballs showered the dragon and he just rolled over with a thunderous sound over and over in the snow.

But what over-awed the man greatly was when the heavens opened and there in the skies did appear the dragons mate Morphusa.

He watched as the dragon did look skyward and call to her. He marvelled at how she circled gracefully before landing by his side.

He was aghast with joy as the people did stroke and cuddle her. And how she did nestle them to her.

To the man there was now great joy of life.

Suddenly the dragon looked towards him and pointed with his wing towards him.

"Ho!" The dragon did shout. "Do you know of this man?" The Dragon asked.

The crowd looked at the man and suddenly they rushed towards him shouting "SANTA! SANTA"

The people crowded around the man and some reached for his hands. Little children tugged at his cape and tunic.

"Listen to them old man. Hear what they say!"

The man listened and he heard words of joy and welcome. But none asked of him other that was he well and would he stay with them. None sought presents or anything of him.

And so that Christmas Santa saw that there was joy and happiness and a reason to believe in.

The man did spend many times with the people and he did receive more from the people than they took from him.

And he saw the kindness that they gave to the dragon.

He did visit with the dragon a few times. And on one visit he found out that the only way to hurt a dragon is to . . . . But that would be telling secrets and Santa never tells a secret.

A DRAGONS TALE

by
Richard Glyndwr Evans

One day a Dragon that was so tall and red did stand at the city gates.

Men, women and children did walk past him.

In their eyes he did see revulsion at his presence.

But he could not move from his post, for he had been commanded to stand there, to watch, listen and wait.

Eventually an old man approached him.

As he neared the great red Dragon, he did reach out his hand to him.

'Walk with me please,' the old man said.

The Dragon did not look at the old man, for he was commanded against doing so.

The old man walked past the Dragon.

'Walk with me now!' the old man commanded.

And so the Dragon did turn and walk a distance behind the man.

Eventually they neared the great forest from whence the Dragon had first come.

'So Dragon!' 'What do you see in people? Other than food!'

The old man chuckled at his little joke, for he knew that Dragons did not eat people.

'I see many wondrous things in them!' Was the reply.

'And yet they treat you so badly!

Do you not wish to display to them your might and power,

To shed your flames and heat upon them? To destroy them?'

The Dragon turned his gaze to the old man.

Not such thoughts have nor can they enter my head and heart for I am to serve and protect them.

Not to cause them pain.

None of my kind are allowed to do such! For we are HIS soldiers!

The old man said to the Dragon that he would leave him where he was, and another would approach soon, but he must wait where he was!

So the Dragon waited, and waited and waited.

Eventually a voice called to him.

'DRAGON! DRAGON! why do you wait when I do summon you?'

The Dragon bowed his head for he knew of the Voice!

'I am told to wait here where I am.'

'Walk with me,' the Voice did say.

So the Dragon did walk forwards towards the voice, but he could see no one.

'Look back Dragon, as you walk.'

The Dragon did so look back and he did see a small etheral black cloaked figure scurrying along behind him.

'Look back to where you go.' He was told by the voice.

'What did you see?'

'I saw a small black cloaked figure, but could not look to it clearly so I do not know who or what it was.' He replied.

'Look again behind you!'

The Dragon turned his head but could see nothing but his tail and all that he had passed.

'What do you see now?'

'I see nothing!'

'You hear my voice, but what do you see or sense?' The Voice Asked.

'I see your warmth and truth and know that you are my Master!' The Dragon stated clearly.

'And I know that I may not raise my eyes to you nor see your Smile for I am unworthy!'

'So!' Said the Voice.

'When you looked back once you saw something vague and yet the second time you saw nothing?'

'Yes Master!'

'The reason you see nothing is that he who was there, is of no substance!

He is nothing, for he has nothing. He gives nothing. He can only take.'

'But the people do not see him and yet they think of him?' the Dragon said with despair. 'And they even call him of my kind, and so only see the horrors that I am!'

'Actually Dragon, they really only see the horrors in you that they are.

For you are but a mirror to them, but they do not know that!

So in truth they do not see you. They only see themselves.'

And with that they did walk and talk until the Dragon found that he was back at the city gates and that all around him children played, laughed and smiled.

And some even cuddled him.

For they saw not the horrors of the non-believer.

Stories of Dragons who watch over you, with Love and Joy that is given to them by GOD, who so loves us all that HE Gave to us HIS Only Begotten Son.

In all who live, there will at times be pain and adversity.
But know that GOD, HIS Angels and Dragons Love you.
That Dragons fight for you and will and do die for you.
That all that matters to Dragons is
Loving and Serving GOD!
And seeing you LIVE!
Be kind to all who near you and
know them for who they truly are!
Love and accept them!
For that is all anyone truly needs!

Printed in Great Britain
by Amazon